For all children exploring who you are:
be playful, be powerful, be proud.
—B. J.

For all trans kids, past and present—
may you always be surrounded by people
who love you for who you are.
—X. C.

Text copyright © 2022 Blue Jaryn. Illustrations copyright © 2022 Xochitl Cornejo. First published in 2022 by Page Street Kids,
an imprint of Page Street Publishing Co., 27 Congress Street, Suite 1511, Salem, MA 01970, www.pagestreetpublishing.com.
All rights reserved. No part of this book may be reproduced or used, in any form or by any means, electronic or mechanical,
without prior permission in writing from the publisher. Distributed by Macmillan, sales in Canada by The Canadian Manda Group.
ISBN-13: 978-1-64567-558-7. ISBN-10: 1-64567-558-0. CIP data for this book is available from the Library of Congress.
This book was typeset in Galvji. The illustrations were created digitally. Cover and book design by Julia Tyler for Page Street Kids.
Edited by Kayla Tostevin for Page Street Kids. Printed and bound in Shenzhen, Guangdong, China.
22 23 24 25 26 CCO 5 4 3 2 1

Page Street Publishing uses only materials from suppliers who are committed to responsible and sustainable forest management.
Page Street Publishing protects our planet by donating to nonprofits like The Trustees, which focuses on local land conservation.

PAYDEN'S PRONOUN PARTY

Blue Jaryn

illustrated by **Xochitl Cornejo**

PAGE STREET KIDS

Payden loved to play dress-up and become **anyone he imagined** . . .

a regal ruler
overseeing a radiant land,

a scientist conducting
startling experiments,

or even a comical puppy frolicking
with Ruffles around the backyard.

But Payden also puzzled about who he really was.

One day, holding tightly onto Ruffles,
Payden tried explaining to his parents,
"I'm not sure I'm a boy . . .
so maybe *he* is not best for me."

"We'll call you whatever you're comfortable with,"
Payden's mother said with a hug.

Payden's father nodded. "Your friends use different pronouns.
Why don't you ask them for advice?"

"Once you decide, we'll throw a big party to celebrate!"
said Payden's mother.

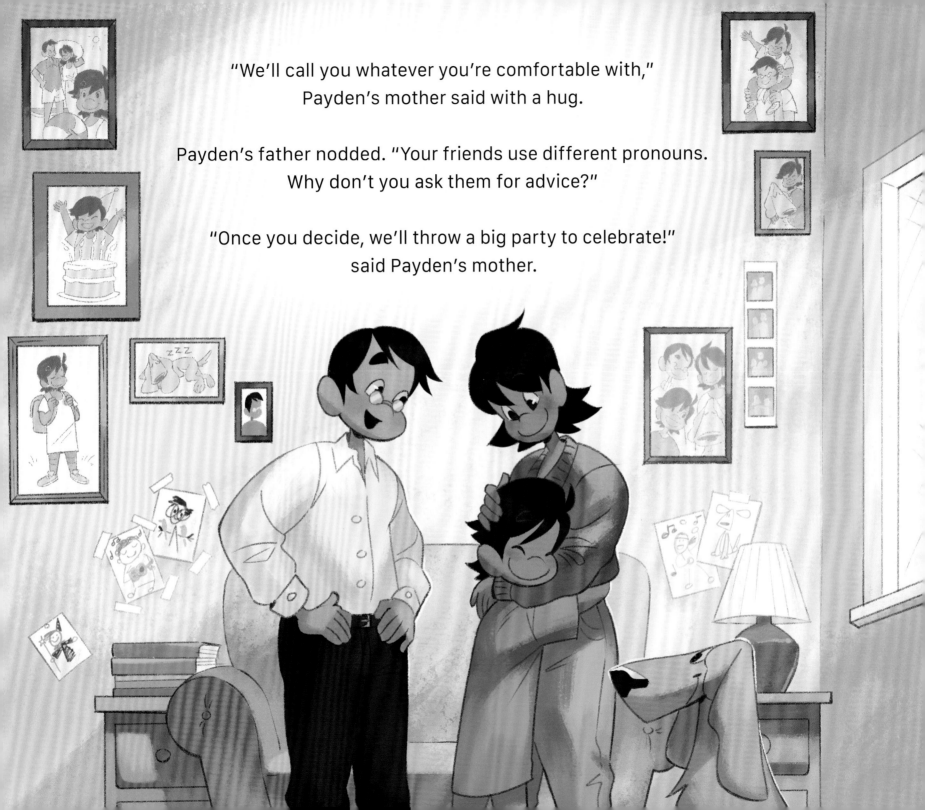

The next day, it was time for Ruffles to visit Hank, the town's vet. Hank cared so much for animals that his clinic was almost a zoo.

"Just as healthy as always," Hank said and tossed Ruffles a treat.

"I was wondering," Payden said, dodging a wayward parrot, "have you always been sure about being a **he**?"

"Hmm, yes, it's always matched for me. Just like being a vet," said Hank. "But I'm glad there are more ways to be than *he* or *she*."

Payden beamed.

"Like all the colors in the rainbow!"

On the way home, Payden called in on Shay, the town's acrobatic artist.
She always painted from a trapeze.

"Hi, Payden! Is something troubling you?" Shay asked.
Payden nodded. "I've been wondering about my gender and pronouns."

"Ah, I understand. It's important to feel your pronouns fit.
People used to think I was a boy, but I've always been a girl.
Now when I hear **she**, I'm flying—just like this!"
Shay swung wildly with her paintbrush.

Payden imagined being called **she**:
*Payden has fun when **she** plays dress-up.*
Instead of flying, Payden felt wobbly,
as if standing on a slippery log.

The following day, Payden visited a friend from school.
Theo was playing a curious trumpet they invented,
one of many in their musical workshop.

"Hey, Theo," Payden said, "what's it
like being called **they**?"

"Well, as I'm not a boy or a girl, I tried out
different pronouns," Theo said, tinkering on
their trumpet. "I realized being called **they**
is like getting the best hug in the world."

Payden imagined someone saying, *Payden loves **their** dog very much*. This was a little like being hugged, but not the best hug in the world.

That afternoon, Payden attended dance class. Another student, Zoe, was working on a new kind of dancing, which hadn't quite won people over. Not that ze minded.

"Hi, Zoe," Payden said. "How did you decide to use **ze** and **she** as your pronouns?"

"Oh, well mostly I feel I'm a girl, but sometimes I don't feel I'm any gender. Both **she** and **ze** feel much more me and make me want to dance!"
Zoe jumped and looped across the room.

Payden imagined someone saying,
Payden believes in **zir** *friend's talent.*
This felt warmer but didn't wholly sound
much more me for Payden.

Back home, Payden played dress-up while trying out different pronouns,

swirling and skipping,

humming and hoping,

puzzling

and pondering . . .

Until finally,
realizing that gender neutral pronouns personally fit best,
Payden discovered the ones that sounded **just right**,
giving a skin-tingling, warm sense of wholeness.

This made Payden feel like flying,

and getting the
best hug in the world,

and dancing all at once.

"I want to be called **e**, **em**, and **eir**, at least for now,"
Payden announced to eir parents.

They were delighted and began to organize the party: a dress-up pronoun party!

All Payden's friends arrived wearing creative and colorful costumes. And pronoun badges too.

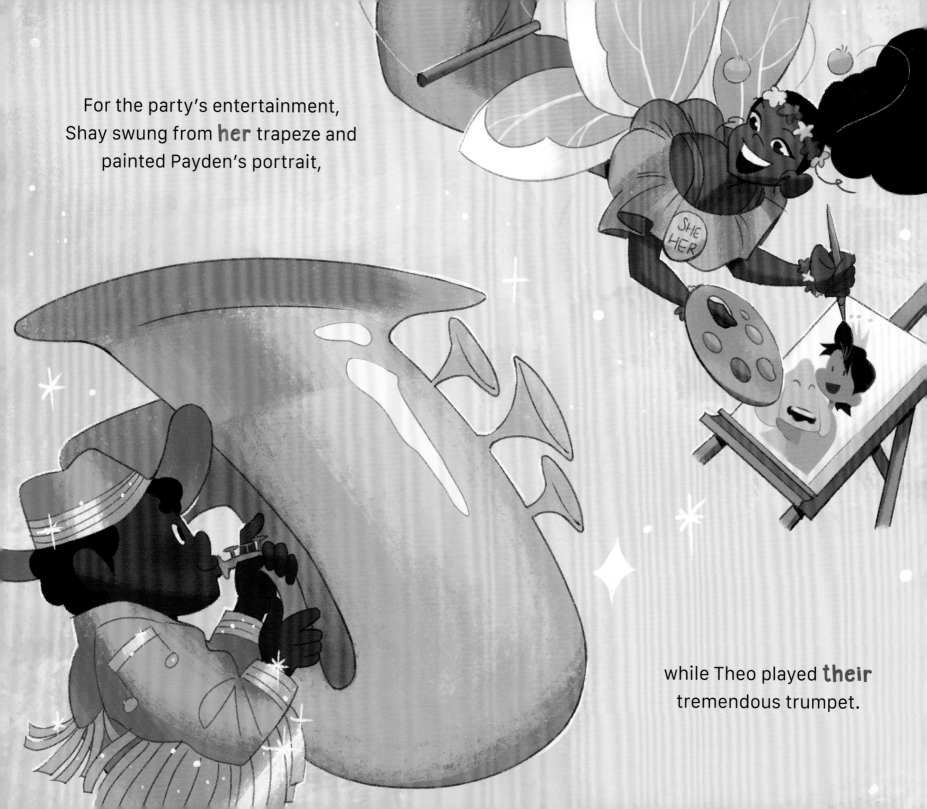

For the party's entertainment, Shay swung from **her** trapeze and painted Payden's portrait,

SHE HER

while Theo played **their** tremendous trumpet.

Hank set up **his** humorous petting zoo, and Zoe zoomed across the stage for **zir** unique dance.

Payden smiled and laughed so much that **eir** face ached.

As the party paraded on into the evening,
Payden hugged Ruffles close and whispered,